THE ADVENTUR...

Bob the Pigeon & Mr Todd

Written
& Illustrated by
# TONY RACE

Based on a true story by **ALAN TODD**

Dedicated to 'My Darling Nan' Mary Wilson

First published in Great Britain as a softback original in 2023

Illustrations © Tony Race

Editing, design, typesetting and publishing by UK Book Publishing

www.ukbookpublishing.com

ISBN: 978-1-915338-88-4

THE ADVENTURES OF

Bob the Pigeon & Mr Todd

Bob is not a street pigeon
picking up crumbs.

You will not see him in a city
with all of his chums.

He will not flock around
you, or fly too close;

And, he doesn't poop on statues
which is good ... I suppose!

Bob is not a Wood
pigeon living in a tree

Billing and cooing and eating
farmers' seed for tea.

He will not spoil your harvest
nor eat all your leaves.

You will never find him in a barn
nor nesting in church eaves.

Bob's a Racing pigeon who flies
long distance in the sky.

If you look up, you may see him on
an adventure - WAY UP HIGH.

He wears an identity bracelet
which you may think is odd

But that is just to let you all know
he's a friend of Mr Todd.

Mr Todd built Bob a nest
which is called a loft.

Betty is Bob's girlfriend and
she's made it nice and soft.

In North East England we
call this nest a cree

And it's just the right size
for a family of three.

Racing day is exciting and
there's always lots to do.

Bob has berries for breakfast
and Mr Todd has a brew.

Bob has time with Betty as he
wants to say goodbye

Then Mr Todd excitedly says,
'Let's go, Bob; time for you to fly.'

Bob and his friends ride to
Portsmouth in a truck

To catch a ferry to Guernsey, Mr
Todd wishes him 'GOOD LUCK'.

When they arrive at the race,
it's quite a celebration,

Then they hear the bell ring ...
it's time for The Liberation.

After Liberation, Bob
flies high into the sky.

From Guernsey he sees England then
France as he's soaring way up high.

Bob knows to fly towards
England as that is his home,

There's DANGER up there in the sky,
BOB IS NOT ALONE!

An Osprey is a bigger bird who
hunts across the sea.

Bob must fly back with extra care
to get back home for tea.

He flies up high into the clouds from
the Osprey's beady stare,

And in the clouds he catches his
breath... he's had a dreadful scare.

As Bob flies down out of the
clouds and takes a look around,

He's flown too high inside the clouds
and cannot see the ground.

The sea is all around him as
far as he can see,

Oh! what a problem; he won't
be home for tea.

Mr Todd and Betty
waited in the cree.

Mr Todd checked his watch
again - Bob was late for tea.

The other pigeons had all flown
home from way across the sea,

Betty and Mr Todd wondered...
Ah. Where can Bob be?

Bob flew around for hours
not seeing any land.

Flying out to sea was
never really planned.

He looked down and spied a boat
where he could rest all day,

But little did he know, it was
bound for the USA!

Bob was so exhausted when
he landed on the boat,

He fell asleep for days and days
and allowed himself to float.

Awoken by a seagull, he asked,
'Where did we go?'

The seagull in a strange voice
said, 'The Gulf of Mexico.'

Bob said to the seagull,
'I need to find dry land.'

The gull replied, 'Just follow me,
I'll take you to the sand.'

Bob flew beyond the sand until the
land looked lush and green

And landed in Alabama, in the prettiest
garden he'd ever seen.

A kind old man gave Bob some
food and a lovely place to stay

And straight away he knew that
Bob had come from far away.

A vet came in from Monroeville
and used Bob's ID bracelet,

Then typed in numbers on her phone...
how easy was that to trace it!

'Hello,' she said to Mr Todd,
'I'm a vet in the USA.

I'm happy to tell you we have
Bob and he's doing okay.'

Mr Todd was overjoyed that
Bob was safe and well,

But how to get him home! Umm.
He just couldn't tell.

Mr Todd went on TV, told
everyone about Bob.

Many people wanted
to help so it really did the job.

The Sun, British Airways and
Anpario PLC made a plan,

To get Bob back to England and
make Mr Todd a happy man.

From Newcastle to London
and on to the USA,

Mr Todd landed in New
Orleans the very next day

Thank you to the vet
and the kind old man

And to everyone who gave
their time to sort out the plan.

Bob the Racing pigeon went
on a plane with Mr Todd

But when they arrived home
they saw something very odd.

A welcome fanfare played and
cameras clicked and flashed

As Bob is now a superstar and
this adventure is not his last.

Bob the pigeon and Mr Todd are
back where they should be

And Bob is safe and happy,
comfortable in his cree.

As Bob and Betty's family
snuggle in their nest

Bob knows that after this adventure,
Home Is the Best.

Dear Mr Todd,

We are going to race in France and we were wondering if Bob would compete by any chance? It's a whole new adventure and promises to be fun!!! Please reply and let me know if you and Bob can come?

H. P Flyer

Club Secretary

THANK YOU

Thank you to all the people and companies for your part in this incredible story.

 Valerie Hadley at IAG Cargo

British Airways

 Ryan Parry at The Sun

Sarah Osborne at Anpario PLC

Swainston Seeds

 Lambournes

Andrew Hartley at BBC LOOK NORTH

 Julia Breen at ITV TYNETEES

Monroeville Animal Shelter

Joanna Echevarria for her guidance and her invaluable friendship

Printed in Great Britain
by Amazon

18850072R00016